The Charmingly Clever Cousin

Princess Power

The Charmingly Clever Cousin

By Suzanne Williams

Illustrated by Chuck Gonzales

HarperTrophy®
An Imprint of HarperCollins*Publishers*

HarperTrophy® is a registered trademark of
HarperCollins Publishers Inc.

The Charmingly Clever Cousin

Library of Congress Cataloging-in-Publication Data is available.
ISBN-10: 0-06-078301-X (trade) — ISBN-13: 978-0-06-078301-3 (trade)
ISBN-10: 0-06-078300-1 (pbk.) — ISBN-13: 978-0-06-078300-6 (pbk.)

Typography by Jennifer Bankenstein
❖
First Harper Trophy edition, 2006
Visit us on the World Wide Web!
www.harpercollinschildrens.com

To Mom and Dad,
with love from their #1 princess

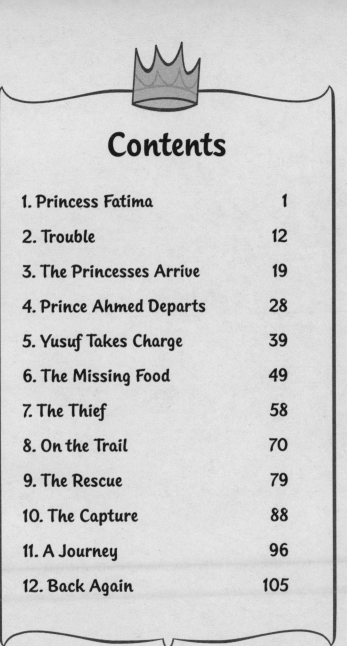

Contents

Princess Fatima

PRINCESS FATIMA SHIFTED IN HER CHAIR AND glanced longingly at her flying carpet leaning against the Royal Nursery wall. She'd give anything to be on her carpet right now, soaring over the countryside.

A soft cry drew her attention to the sleeping baby in her lap. Fatima studied her nephew's bald head. It looked like a squashed pumpkin and was much too big for his body.

Drool wet his chin. When he was awake, all Prince Hassim did was burp, spit up, and cry. *Boring.*

Fatima wondered what her friends—the princesses Lysandra, Elena, and Tansy—were doing right now. Two months had passed since they'd first met. Two *l-o-n-g* months. Whatever her princess friends were up to had to be a lot more exciting than this.

Fatima sighed. She didn't really like babysitting, but she hadn't wanted to refuse when her sister, Selime, had asked for her help. After all, Fatima didn't get to see Selime very often. Even by flying carpet, it took two whole days to reach the palace where her sister and brother-in-law, Prince Ahmed, lived.

Rising carefully so as not to wake him, Fatima carried Hassim to his Royal Cradle.

Laying the sleeping baby down, she tiptoed away. With any luck, maybe he'd nap for a couple of hours. Then she'd be free to do something fun for a change. Perhaps she could even get out of the palace for a while.

Fatima glanced at her carpet again. Would it be so wrong to take a quick flight into town and spend a few minutes wandering through the bazaar? She hadn't flown anywhere in the past two weeks. She longed to run her fingers through the colorful silk scarves and sample the honeyed stuffed dates the merchants sold.

But even as Fatima thought about leaving, a stern voice echoed inside her head. It was Prince Ahmed's voice, scolding her for nearly dropping baby Hassim when she had run with him down the hall last night. She'd only wanted to be in time to see the acrobats perform in the Grand Hall before dinner!

Later, when she came to Ahmed and Selime's room to apologize, she'd overheard him talking with her sister. "Fatima is much too young and irresponsible to take care of Hassim," he'd declared.

Hidden behind the door, Fatima had imagined the frown on his less-than-handsome face, with eyebrows that were too bushy and a nose that was somewhat pointed. Prince Ahmed was no Prince Charming—except, of course, to her sister.

"She's twelve," Selime had said. "That's old enough."

"For some girls, perhaps," Ahmed had replied. "But Fatima is too impulsive. She does things without considering if her actions could be dangerous. Hassim could get hurt!"

"Babies are always getting hurt," Selime had said calmly. "Why, just the other day, he grabbed at my tiara while I was holding him and scratched his little arm."

Fatima felt a rush of gratitude toward her sister for sticking up for her. Honestly! Prince Ahmed was *so* overprotective. When it came to Hassim, he was fussier than a mother hen with her chicks. Instead of apologizing, Fatima had turned on her heels and gone back to her room.

Now, a knock on the Royal Nursery door made Fatima jump. She hurried to open it. "Shh," she said to the kitchen maid standing outside. "Prince Hassim is asleep."

The kitchen maid was a skinny girl with rosy cheeks. As she lowered her eyes and curtsied, her long, dark pigtail fell over one shoulder. "Pardon me, Princess. The Royal Chef sent me to ask what you'd like for lunch."

A large helping of free time, Fatima almost said. Then an idea popped into her head. "What's your name?" she asked.

"Nar, Your Highness," the girl replied.

"How old are you, Nar?"

"Fourteen."

Fatima nodded. If *she*, at twelve, was old enough to watch a baby, surely a girl of fourteen was even better. Besides, it would only be for a short while.

A few minutes later Fatima sailed through the Royal Nursery window on her flying carpet, headed for the bazaar. Nar had been only too happy to watch Hassim. She'd sunk into a chair and put up her feet, obviously glad for a chance to rest.

The wind rippled through Fatima's silk blouse and tossed her long hair as she skillfully guided her carpet toward town. Swooping over roofs and colorful lines of laundry that flapped in the breeze, Fatima inhaled the fresh, sweet air and relaxed. She could fly as easily as a fish could swim.

Just outside the tents of the bazaar, Fatima landed under a large palm tree. She rolled up her flying carpet, strapped it onto her back, and strode barefoot into the bazaar. It buzzed with the sounds of shouting merchants, haggling customers, squawking chickens, and bawling camels.

Pushing through crowds of turbaned men and perfumed women, Fatima made her way from one end of the bazaar to the other. Along the way she admired bolts of satin, carpets, and colorful silk scarves. It would've been even more fun if her friends had been with her. Together they might have stumbled upon an adventure, like when they'd found the frog prince in the marketplace near Lysandra's castle.

Hungry because she hadn't eaten lunch, Fatima bought some dates sweetened with honey and stuffed with almonds. They were delicious! Licking her fingers, she sighed with contentment. It was wonderful to escape from the palace. But Fatima supposed she'd better get back since she'd promised Nar she wouldn't be gone long.

On her way out of the bazaar, a display of beautiful leather sandals caught Fatima's eye. She didn't usually wear shoes of any kind, but these sandals were fabulous! The leather bands were carved with intricate designs of birds and flowers.

"Go ahead. Try them on," coaxed the merchant.

Fatima did. But choosing just the right pair, and getting the merchant to agree to a fair price, took a while longer than she'd expected. By the time she flew back to the palace, the sun was noticeably lower in the sky than when she'd left. Still, she couldn't have been gone longer than a couple of hours. With any luck, baby Hassim would still be asleep, or just waking up.

In her hurry to get back, Fatima whooshed through the Royal Nursery window. Her carpet came to an abrupt halt, and she tumbled off. Jumping to her feet, Fatima turned around, hoping Nar hadn't noticed her less-than-perfect landing.

But the kitchen maid *had* noticed. So had the Royal Chef and, worst of all, Prince Ahmed. Nar glanced away, tears running down her cheeks. The Royal Chef scratched his head in confusion. And Prince Ahmed? He scowled at Fatima, looking as angry as a spitting camel.

Trouble

"HOW COULD YOU!" YELLED PRINCE AHMED, his face bright red. "We trusted you to look after Hassim!"

Fatima's eyes darted to Hassim's cradle. It was empty! Her voice shook as she asked, "Where is he? Has he been kidnapped?"

"He's with Selime in our room," Prince Ahmed said more calmly. "The poor tyke. He was very upset when he woke up and you weren't here."

"Really?" Fatima hadn't thought it would make any difference to Hassim who took care of him.

"I'm sorry, Princess," Nar wailed. "I tried to comfort the babe—really I did. I don't think he likes me. He wouldn't stop crying. And when I put him up on my shoulder, he went stiff and started to scream. The whole palace heard him."

"It's not your fault," said Fatima. Prince Hassim had probably only been suffering from gas and needed to have his tummy rubbed. "I shouldn't have asked you to take my place."

The Royal Chef waved his hands in the air. "And now dinner will be late! We have much to do in the kitchen."

"Of course," said Prince Ahmed. "I'm sorry for keeping you here so long. You may go."

After they'd left, Ahmed turned back to Fatima. "I'd like an explanation for your behavior," he said with a frown. "But I think Selime would like to hear it too."

Fatima gulped. She could handle Ahmed's anger, but she hated to disappoint her sister—or to think that something bad could've happened to little baby Hassim. Nevertheless, she followed Ahmed down the hall.

Selime was singing to Hassim in her beautiful voice as he lay gurgling in her lap. He seemed to have gotten over his fright quickly enough, thought Fatima.

Prince Ahmed sat beside Selime and tickled Hassim's tummy. "How's my sweet little baby waby?" he cooed. "How's my little princey wincey?"

Fatima nearly gagged. Baby talk was so disgusting!

Selime swept back her wavy hair as she raised her head to look at Fatima. "Are you unhappy here?" she asked, a hurt look in her eyes.

"N-no," said Fatima. "And I'm sorry about what happened, only . . ." She paused, not wanting to say that she'd been bored, in case she hurt her sister's feelings even more.

Prince Ahmed frowned. "Only what?"

"Only . . . bats and bullfrogs!" she blurted. "Sometimes I just need to get out of the palace for a while!"

Prince Ahmed's forehead wrinkled. "Please don't curse. It's not nice. You could have said you needed time off. You're not exactly a prisoner here."

"I know. But I'm supposed to be looking after Prince Hassim, and—"

"And you didn't feel that you could ask for some time away from him," finished Selime.

Fatima nodded miserably. Now her sister would know she didn't find babysitting to be all that interesting.

But to her surprise, Selime said, "Being cooped up all day with a baby would be hard for any young girl. I expect you'd like the company of princesses your own age. How would you like to invite a few of your friends to visit?"

Fatima's face brightened. "Could I? I mean, would it be all right?"

Selime smiled at her husband. "You wouldn't mind, would you, dear? Fatima needs a break, and I can handle Hassim by myself for a while."

"Well," Prince Ahmed said slowly, "I

suppose that would be all right. For a little while, anyway."

"Yes!" shouted Fatima. Excited at the thought of seeing her friends, she hugged Selime. But to Ahmed she only said, "Thanks."

The Princesses Arrive

Several days later the princesses arrived. Fatima was watching for them and raced from her room to the front of the palace when their carriages rolled up.

"Wow! This place is beautiful!" exclaimed Tansy, giving Fatima a hug. At nine, Tansy was the youngest of Fatima's friends. She had lots of freckles and ginger-colored hair.

"Yes, I suppose it is." Fatima tried to see

things as Tansy must see them—the smooth, polished marble of the palace walls, the ornate columns, the high, arched doorways. It *was* a nice place, especially when you could leave it from time to time.

"Hi, Fatima. Long time, no see!" Lysandra's wavy blond hair sparkled as the sunlight

streamed through the windows. She was ten, two years younger than Fatima. Fatima would always feel grateful to her for hosting the talent show auditions that had brought the four princesses together.

Fatima hugged Elena next. She was eleven, with soft, hazel eyes and frizzy brown

hair. Together the four girls entered the Grand Hall, where Ahmed, Selime, and Hassim were waiting to meet them.

Fatima introduced her friends. Standing tall and looking graceful, Selime smiled at the princesses. "It's good to meet you," she said. "Fatima has told me a lot about you. I hope you'll have a lovely time while you're here."

"Yes," Prince Ahmed said stiffly. "But I hope you'll try not to make too much noise while Hassim is napping."

Fatima rolled her eyes, but the others didn't seem offended.

Elena bent over baby Hassim. "He's adorable." Gurgling, Hassim reached out and grabbed a handful of Elena's frizzy hair. She gently untangled the strands from his fist, not seeming to mind at all.

Lysandra let Hassim curl his tiny hand around one of her fingers. "What a cutie!" she exclaimed. "Maybe Gabriella will have a baby soon, and I'll be an auntie too." Gabriella was Lysandra's older sister. She'd gotten married not long ago to Prince Jerome, the frog prince the girls had rescued from the market-place. All four princesses had attended the wedding.

Adorable? thought Fatima. A cutie? Hadn't they noticed Hassim's bald, squashed-pumpkin head? Maybe Lysandra and Elena were just being nice; Tansy hadn't paid much attention to him. But then Fatima remembered that Tansy had six brothers. She was probably tired of boys.

After lunch the girls went for a flying carpet ride. Fatima steered the carpet over the palace's gleaming towers and lush gardens, and past a small lake. They skimmed above the striped tents of the bazaar, then circled the vast and windswept desert that lay beyond the boundaries of town.

"Traveling by carpet is the *only* way to go," gushed Lysandra. "What a fantastic view!"

On their return, Fatima spied a splendid black stallion standing just outside the palace gates. As the carpet drew closer, she could see that the stallion's saddle was covered in velvet and embroidered with gold thread. "I recognize that horse!" she cried. "Yusuf must've just arrived!"

"Who's Yusuf?" asked Tansy.

"My brother-in-law's cousin," Fatima explained. "Only he's not a bit like Ahmed. Yusuf's charming and clever, and . . . well, I just know you'll like him."

Fatima guided the flying carpet over the palace gates and landed close to the front entrance. The princesses climbed off. Then Fatima hurriedly rolled up the carpet and led her friends into the palace.

She had expected to find Yusuf in the Grand Hall, sipping tea and telling stories, but he wasn't there. Fatima frowned. "I wonder where he could be?"

"I bet your sister would know," Elena suggested.

"Good idea," said Fatima. "Let's go find her."

The girls started through the wing of the palace that led to Ahmed and Selime's room. Tansy gaped at the silk tapestries that hung from the marble walls. "Ahmed and your sister must be very rich," she said.

Fatima snorted. "All of Ahmed's money

comes from his father, King Murad. The king *gave* Ahmed this palace as a wedding present. Ahmed's an only child. When King Murad dies, Ahmed will become king and inherit everything. Then he and Selime will be *very* wealthy."

As the princesses neared Ahmed's library, they heard voices. "Yusuf's in here!" Fatima said excitedly. "Come on!"

Without bothering to knock, she pushed open the door. Yusuf, handsome as ever, looked up from the sofa where he sat beside Selime. His flashing, dark eyes lit up, and the corners of his mouth curled into a smile beneath an elegant mustache. "Fatima!" he exclaimed. "My favorite cousin-in-law! How's the princess biz? Kiss any frogs yet?"

Fatima blushed. "Not yet."

The other girls giggled. Yusuf winked at them. "And who might these beauties be?"

Fatima introduced her friends. Then she noticed how worried Ahmed and Selime looked. "Is something the matter?" she asked.

Staring into his lap, Ahmed said nothing.

But Selime sniffled into a lace handkerchief. "King Murad is ill. He may even be dying!"

Prince Ahmed Departs

FATIMA HUGGED HER SISTER. SHE KNEW Selime was very fond of her father-in-law. He shared her love of music, and they often sang duets together during visits.

Yusuf stopped smiling, and the joking tone left his voice. "That's right," he said gravely. "And I'm afraid I'm the bearer of the bad news."

Looking up, Ahmed said, "Perhaps he's not as ill as he thinks."

Yusuf sighed. "How I wish that were true."

Ahmed tapped his fingers on the arm of his chair. He seemed to be thinking. "I know my father well," he said finally. "If he gets even a small scratch on his hand, he thinks he's at death's door."

Tansy nodded. "One of my brothers is like that. Every time Ethan coughs, he's sure he's coming down with the plague."

Yusuf frowned at her. "I'm afraid it's different this time," he said to Ahmed. "The doctors say there's nothing they can do for him."

"Doctors can be wrong," Elena said softly.

Ahmed nodded, but his face fell. "I must go to him. I hope there's been a mistake, though. My father worries a lot, but he's always been as healthy and strong as an ogre."

Yusuf gave him a pitying look. "We can

only pray that you're right."

"Amen," murmured Lysandra.

Ahmed rose to his feet. "I'll leave first thing tomorrow morning."

"And I'll go with you!" Yusuf declared.

"Thank you," Ahmed said gratefully. "I'd welcome your company."

Poor Ahmed, thought Fatima. She'd feel awful if her own father were dreadfully ill. She glanced at Selime, who was twisting her handkerchief nervously. Poor Ahmed *and* Selime.

For dinner that night there was peacock in raisin sauce, peas, creamed potatoes, apple tarts, and stuffed figs. Everything tasted delicious, as always. But in spite of the Royal Chef's efforts, the only one who seemed to have much of an appetite was Yusuf. Fatima supposed he must not have had much to eat during his long ride to the palace. She watched as he tore off a huge hunk of bread, then swished it around his plate to soak up the raisin sauce.

"I wish you were staying longer," she said.

Yusuf grinned at her. "Who knows? You might just get your wish." Popping the bread into his mouth, he chewed vigorously.

"Really? You mean you aren't going to travel with Ahmed after all?"

Yusuf patted her shoulder. "Sorry, Princess. I have to go. But I'll try to come back as soon as I can. Then I just might stay so long you'll *want* to get rid of me."

Fatima smiled. "You could never stay that long."

Yusuf wiped the raisin sauce from his mustache and glanced at the other princesses. "I wonder if your friends would agree," he said playfully.

The three princesses giggled. "Can't say yet," answered Tansy. "But if I can live with six brothers, I guess I could stand being around you for a while."

Yusuf roared with laughter.

"He's certainly cheerful, isn't he?" Lysandra whispered to Elena.

Elena shrugged. "Maybe he's just trying to make up for the bad news."

After dinner Selime and Ahmed excused themselves from the table. Selime wanted to bathe Hassim and put him to bed, and Ahmed needed to make preparations for the next day's journey.

Yusuf entertained the princesses with stories about dragons, fairies, and ogres. Then he showed them some tricks he claimed to have learned from a traveling magician. The girls burst into laughter when he drew a hard-boiled egg from Tansy's ear and made strands of Lysandra's blond hair dance in the air like a snake. When he waved his hand in front of Elena's eyes and turned them from hazel to blue to hazel again, the princesses were amazed.

"How did you do that?" Fatima asked.

Yusuf smoothed his mustache. "A magician never reveals his secrets," he said mysteriously. Then, out of thin air, he produced a huge bouquet of red roses. "For my four beauties," he said, handing a rose to each princess.

Fatima sniffed her flower. "It smells wonderful."

"It sure does," said Lysandra, burying her nose in the petals. "Thank you."

Yusuf bowed again. "You're welcome, my dears. And now I must say good night, since tomorrow will be a long day." And with that,

he vanished in a puff of smoke.

"Wow!" said Tansy. "Is he really gone?"

"He can't be," said Lysandra. "Let's look for him."

The princesses searched under the table and behind the curtains, but finally they gave up. Yawning, they left the hall and went to bed.

When Fatima awoke the next morning, she heard noises outside her window. Yusuf's and Ahmed's horses stood in front of the palace. They pawed the ground and tossed their heads, impatient to be off.

Fatima woke the others. The four princesses dressed quickly and ran down the hall to say good-bye to the two men. They were just in time to hear Ahmed say to Selime, "Don't worry. I'm sure it can't be as bad as the doctors say. I'll probably be back tomorrow night." Ahmed lifted Hassim from Selime's arms and hugged him. "Take good care of your mommy, my little sonny wunny."

Fatima made a face. She guessed it was too much to hope that her friends hadn't heard.

Yusuf appeared from the opposite hallway.

He smiled when he saw the girls. "How nice of you to see us off."

Prince Ahmed frowned. "I wish I wasn't going to be gone while you and your friends are here," he said to Fatima. "You be sure to mind your sister."

Bats and bullfrogs! Fatima's face grew warm. Ahmed treated her as if she were an infant. And in front of everyone, too!

"The princesses will be great company for Selime and Hassim while we're gone," said Yusuf. "And I'm sure Fatima will be a big help."

Fatima flashed him a smile. Yusuf was so much nicer than Ahmed! If only her brother-in-law could be more like him. It was hard to believe the two men were related. Yet Fatima knew that Yusuf's father, who had died in battle many years ago, had been King Murad's brother.

Everyone followed Ahmed and Yusuf to the palace gates. Shouting "Good-bye" and "See you again soon," the men swung themselves onto their horses and galloped away.

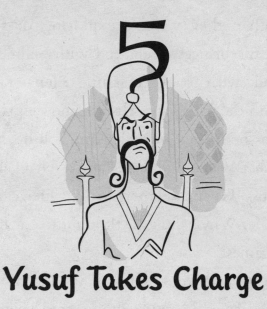

Yusuf Takes Charge

WHILE AHMED AND YUSUF WERE GONE, THE princesses explored the palace and shopped in the bazaar. They returned with scarves and ribbons and treats, such as the honeyed stuffed dates Fatima loved so much. Lysandra insisted on paying for all their purchases with the golden coins from the magical purse she wore around her neck—a purse that never went empty.

When they weren't exploring or shopping, the princesses chatted with Selime and played with baby Hassim. Elena taught Hassim the pat-a-cake rhyme, and he grinned when she helped him clap and roll his hands together. Watching them, Fatima felt a pang of jealousy. Hassim seemed to like Elena better than her. Why hadn't *she* thought to teach him any games?

"I'm worried," Selime announced when Ahmed failed to return home the evening of the second day. She had just put Hassim to bed, and the princesses were sitting by the fountain in the courtyard, gazing at the stars. "What if King Murad is more ill than we thought?"

"Maybe Ahmed just got a late start back,"

Fatima said, hoping to reassure her sister. "He'll probably arrive while we're sleeping."

"I'm sure you're right," said Selime. "I'll try not to fret."

To take their minds off Ahmed's absence, Elena read some poetry and Tansy played her magic flute. Tansy's fingers danced over the holes, creating a lively melody. Everyone's thoughts drifted above them like wispy clouds. *I see the Big Dipper*, Elena

thought. *It looks the same here as it does at home.*

Selime thought, *I wish Ahmed were here.*

Fatima blushed to hear herself think, *I can't wait to see Yusuf again.*

When Lysandra thought, *I'm pooped. I hope we go to bed soon,* Tansy set down her flute.

Selime smiled. Stretching gracefully, she said, "It *is* late. Let's all go to bed. We'll see Ahmed and Yusuf in the morning."

But by breakfast the next day, the men had *still* not arrived. "Maybe we should fly out and search for them," Lysandra suggested after the princesses had eaten.

"Good idea," said Fatima. But as she was unrolling her carpet, hoofbeats sounded outside the window. Yusuf galloped into view on his splendid black stallion.

"Whoa!" he shouted, reining in his horse.

Dropping the carpet, Fatima raced outside with her friends. Yusuf barely had time to climb down from his horse before the girls crowded around him.

"Hey, give a guy some room to breathe," he complained. But then he smiled widely. "I guess you missed me."

Fatima's cheeks warmed, and the other princesses giggled.

Selime appeared in the doorway with Hassim. Her brow wrinkled with concern. "Where's Ahmed? Isn't he with you?"

The corners of Yusuf's mouth curved downward. "Prince Ahmed is attending to King Murad. I'm afraid he may be away for several weeks until . . ." He paused, dropping his eyes. "I fear I was right, Princess. The king will not recover."

Selime's hand flew to her mouth. "No!" she wailed.

Yusuf pulled a piece of paper from his pocket. Bowing, he handed it to Selime. "As you can see from this letter, my cousin has asked me to look after his affairs here at the palace while he's gone."

Selime scanned the letter and sighed. "It's just as you say. There is nothing we can do now but hope and wait. I shall be glad of your help while Ahmed is away."

Yusuf smiled. "Wonderful!" Ordering a groom to look after his horse, he strode into the palace ahead of everyone.

Fatima had hoped Yusuf would entertain her and her friends with more magic tricks now that he was back. But Yusuf took his new duties quite seriously, and he had a lot of ideas for how to run the palace. None of the princesses knew he'd fired any servants until the Royal Chef cornered Selime in the nursery. "How can I operate a kitchen with just one maid and one pastry chef!" he exclaimed indignantly.

Covering her own surprise, Selime assured the Royal Chef she'd look into the matter. "Just what does Yusuf think he's doing?" she fumed after the Royal Chef stormed away. "Ahmed would never have done such a thing!"

Fatima had been just as shocked, but now she came to Yusuf's defense. "He must have his reasons. Let's go talk to him." Her friends said they would go for a walk while Selime and Fatima met with Yusuf.

They found him in Ahmed's library, sitting behind Ahmed's desk. "Ah," Yusuf said, looking up from some papers. "I expect you're wondering why I've let some of the servants go."

Selime nodded, her lips a tight line.

Yusuf smoothed his mustache. "This palace has been very inefficiently run. The servants have grown lazy. Why, one servant could easily do the work of two, or even *three*. Just think of how much money you'll save for other things!"

Saving money sounded like a good idea, but Fatima couldn't help remembering how tired Nar had seemed the afternoon she'd watched Hassim. How could anyone do the jobs of two or three people when just *one* job was tiring?

"King Murad has been very generous," said Selime. "We have as much money as we need."

Yusuf cocked his head. "Really?" He pointed to the ceiling. "See that chandelier? It's very old-fashioned. The new ones are much smarter looking." He paused, examining the room. "And white marble is so . . . so *common*. All the best palaces have been remodeled with black or red."

"I happen to like white marble," Selime said stiffly. "And that chandelier is an *antique*."

Yusuf frowned. "I could say something about your taste, but I won't." Then he smiled broadly. "Change is difficult, isn't it? I understand how uncomfortable all this must be for you. But remember, Prince Ahmed asked me to look after things. Believe me, I only have your best interests at heart."

Did he? Fatima wanted to believe him, but this new Yusuf was someone she didn't know. Where was the old Yusuf who told stories, did magic tricks, and teased her about frogs? "May I ask a favor?" she asked.

"Yes, yes. What is it?" Yusuf said crossly. He sounded as if he was in a hurry to get rid of them.

"Would you please tell us a story after dinner tonight?"

Yusuf rolled his eyes. "Really, Fatima. I'm much too busy for stories these days."

Biting her lip, Fatima tried not to show her disappointment. Yusuf had changed.

The Missing Food

Dinner was served an hour late that night. Fatima sipped her soup slowly. It seemed thinner than usual, with fewer potatoes and carrots and hardly any meat at all. Fatima wondered if this was another of Yusuf's cost-saving ideas, or if the Royal Chef simply hadn't had time to prepare the soup properly with so little staff.

Nar, who didn't usually serve at the

table, hurried back and forth from the kitchen bringing platters of cold chicken and mashed potatoes, and clearing away the dirty dishes. Fatima was glad Yusuf hadn't fired Nar, but she couldn't help noticing how exhausted Nar looked. Her face was red and sweaty, and her long pigtail had become straggly.

Dessert, when it finally came, was a rather lumpy pudding. Fatima noticed Selime left hers untouched, but Yusuf ate heartily. Perhaps he didn't notice the difference in the quality of the food.

Fatima sighed. Why had Yusuf changed so much? Or maybe he had always been this way, and she had never noticed before. If only she knew what was going on inside his head!

Wait a minute, she thought. If Tansy played her flute, they'd *hear* what Yusuf was thinking.

Leaning over, Fatima whispered into Tansy's ear. Tansy grinned. "Sure. Why not?"

Fatima stood. "Isn't it wonderful? Tansy has agreed to play a few tunes for our after-dinner entertainment."

Selime's eyebrows rose. Fatima caught her eye and winked.

Rising from the table, Yusuf said, "I'd love to stay, but I have much to do." He bowed to Tansy. "I'm sorry, Princess. I'm sure your playing is quite lovely."

"Please don't go," Fatima said quickly. "Tansy's worked so hard on her pieces. Haven't you Tansy?"

Tansy nodded and did her best to look sad. Elena and Lysandra exchanged glances. Fatima was pretty sure they'd figured out what she was up to.

Luckily Yusuf didn't know Tansy's flute was magic. Sighing impatiently, he said, "Well, all right. But I can only stay for one song." He sat back down.

Tansy pulled her flute from her pocket and began to play. *Now maybe we'll find out what's really going on,* Fatima heard herself think. The thought popped out before she could stop it.

She glanced at Yusuf. For a second he seemed startled. Then his eyes took on a hooded look. Suddenly the music stopped. Tansy's fingers continued to move over the holes, but the flute made no sound. Tansy frowned. Holding her flute at arm's length, she shook it. But when she put it up to her lips again, it still wouldn't play.

Tansy ran a hand through her hair. "I'm sorry. I don't know what's wrong with my flute. This has never happened before!"

"I'm sorry too, Princess," Yusuf said. "I'm sure I would've enjoyed your little concert.

But now I really must go."

Before he could leave, however, shouting broke out in the Royal Kitchen. A door burst open, and Nar raced into the Grand Hall. Sobbing, she ran straight to Selime. "Don't believe him, Your Highness!" she pleaded. "I'm an honest girl. I wouldn't do a thing like that!" She buried her face in Selime's shoulder.

"Here, here!" Yusuf said loudly. "What is the meaning of this?"

Now the Royal Chef ran in, huffing and puffing, and red in the face. Bending over to catch his breath, he pointed at Nar. "She's a thief!"

Fatima gasped. Please don't let it be true, she thought. She rather liked Nar and felt sorry the maid had to work so hard.

"Really?" said Yusuf. "What has she stolen?"

The Royal Chef wiped his face with a handkerchief. "Food," he said. "Leftovers. A

whole roast beef from last night's dinner."

Selime smoothed Nar's long pigtail. "Did you actually *see* her take anything?" she asked mildly.

"Well, no," the Royal Chef admitted, "but who else could have done it? It wasn't me, and the pastry chef has been home ill the last two nights." He looked hard at Yusuf. "There are only three of us left to

run the kitchen, you know."

Yusuf laughed. "I bet it wasn't the girl at all. I bet *rats* have been stealing the food."

"Rats!" spluttered the Royal Chef. "How dare you, sir! I keep a very clean kitchen."

"Of course you do," Selime soothed.

If Nar *had* stolen any food, thought Fatima, she must've been hungry. The maid had been working harder than ever lately. As everyone knows, hard work increases your appetite.

Fatima spoke up. "Forgive me," she said, "but *I* took the food."

"What?" Yusuf and the Royal Chef shouted at the same time.

"I . . . well . . . I got hungry in the middle of the night," Fatima lied.

"But a *whole* roast?" the Royal Chef asked doubtfully.

Elena caught Fatima's eye. "It was for all of us," she said. "We were *all* hungry."

"That's right," said Lysandra. "We decided to have a midnight snack."

Tansy rubbed her belly. "That roast was *delicious*!"

Fatima glanced at the Royal Chef. "Sorry we didn't tell you. I guess we should have known better."

"Humph." Grumbling under his breath,

the Royal Chef stomped back to the kitchen.

Yusuf eyed Fatima. "Nice try," he said. "I honestly believed the problem was rats, but now I smell a cover-up. I went to bed at midnight last night, and when I passed your room, it was completely dark and quiet."

He turned to face Nar as she raised her tear-stained face from Selime's shoulder. Pointing a long, slender finger at her, Yusuf said coolly, "You're fired."

The Thief

Sobbing, Nar fled the Grand Hall. The princesses ran after her.

"Don't worry, Nar!" Fatima cried. "I'll find a way to convince Yusuf to hire you back. Who cares about a missing roast?"

"But you don't understand!" wailed Nar. "I didn't steal it!"

"Honest?" said Lysandra.

"I'm sure it's fine if you did," said Tansy.

"You were probably hungry."

Nar crossed her arms and glared at the princesses. "You don't believe me."

Fatima blinked. "You mean you *didn't* steal that chicken?"

"No!" shouted Nar. "That's what I've been trying to tell you!"

"Then I wonder who, or what, did?" said Elena, frowning.

Nar shook her head. "I wish I knew. But I know it wasn't any rat. I'm the one scrubbing the kitchen each night now that the girl who used to do it is gone. The Royal Chef won't let me leave till the whole kitchen sparkles like dew."

Fatima put her arm around Nar's shoulder. "We're sorry we didn't believe you," she said. "We do now, and we're going to prove you didn't take that food."

Nar's eyes widened. "How will you do that?"

Fatima smiled at her friends. "We'll find a way to catch the *real* thief!"

That night, long after everyone else had gone to bed, the princesses sneaked into the kitchen and hid in the pantry. Fatima left the door open a crack so they could keep an eye on the entrance to the cold cellar.

Lysandra yawned. "How long do you

think we'll have to wait?" she whispered.

"I don't know," Fatima admitted. She hoped she wasn't keeping the others up for nothing.

"Shh," said Tansy, cocking her head. "I think I hear something."

The princesses froze. Footsteps sounded in the hallway. The kitchen door swung open and a cloaked figure crept into the room.

Fatima strained to see the intruder's face, but it was hidden by a hood.

Holding their breaths, the princesses watched the stranger go down into the cellar. In a few minutes he—or maybe it was a *she*— reappeared, carrying that evening's leftover chicken. The stranger set the bird on the kitchen table, then disappeared into the cellar a second time, bringing up more leftovers. After cramming the food into a bag, the thief slung it over a shoulder. The bag caught at the cloak, and the hood fell back.

Yusuf? Fatima covered her mouth so he wouldn't hear her gasp. What was he up to? And how dare he fire Nar when *he* was the one stealing the food! Fatima was about to push open the pantry door and confront him when she remembered what Ahmed had said: *Fatima is too impulsive. She does things without considering if her actions could be dangerous.*

But Yusuf wouldn't hurt her or any of the others, would he? Fatima bit her lip. She didn't know what this Yusuf, this *changed* Yusuf, would or wouldn't do. Holding a finger to her lips to caution the others, Fatima waited until Yusuf left the room.

When the palace doors clanged shut, the princesses crept out of the pantry and ran to Fatima's room. From her window, they watched Yusuf load the stolen food into his horse's saddlebags.

"I wonder where he's going with all that food?" Elena asked.

Tansy tapped her foot impatiently. "We won't know unless we follow him."

"What's keeping us?" said Lysandra. "Let's go!"

But Fatima stopped them. "Let's wait. If

Yusuf is back by morning, maybe he'll explain what's going on. Anyway, waiting will give us more time to think." That's what Ahmed would want her to do if he were here, she thought.

They watched as Yusuf swung a leg over his horse and galloped away. Lysandra looked worried. "And what if he *doesn't* come back?"

"He will," Fatima said. "He's got too many ideas for running this palace *not* to come back."

Sure enough, when the princesses arrived for breakfast late the next morning, Yusuf was finishing a large cheese omelette. "Morning, Princesses," he said. "I trust you slept well."

Fatima raised an eyebrow. "Fine, thanks. How about you?"

"Like a baby," said Yusuf. He patted his mouth with a napkin, missing a bit of egg on his mustache. "Now, if you'll excuse me, I have work to do." He rose from the table.

Fatima frowned, but decided not to mention seeing him last night. Not yet, anyway. Angry that he'd lied, she decided not to tell him about the egg on his mustache, either.

After Yusuf left, the princesses sat down to eat. "Yusuf is up to something for sure," said Lysandra. "If he sneaks out again tonight, I say we follow him."

Before Fatima could reply, the Royal Chef burst into the room. Dropping a tray of muffins on the table, he rushed back to the kitchen before Fatima could even thank him. She reached for a poppy seed muffin. "We'll take my flying carpet. The dark should help to hide us."

Tansy took a blueberry muffin. "Sounds good."

With a thoughtful expression on her face, Elena remarked, "I've been wondering about that letter."

"What letter?" asked Lysandra.

"The one Yusuf gave Selime. He said Ahmed wrote it. Do you suppose she still has it?"

Fatima stared at her. "Are you thinking Ahmed *didn't* write that letter?"

"I don't know," Elena said honestly. "But if you think Selime wouldn't mind, maybe we could take a look at it."

"Let's go!" Fatima said, jumping up from the table.

The princesses found Selime in her room, playing with Hassim. When they told her what they wanted, Selime searched in her desk for Ahmed's letter while Elena held the baby. He squealed and gurgled happily in her arms.

"Here it is," said Selime, handing Fatima

the letter. "I don't like the changes Yusuf has been making either. But I'm afraid this was definitely written by Ahmed. I know his handwriting."

Fatima read the letter as Lysandra and Tansy looked over her shoulder:

My dear Selime,

I am detained. Against my will, I'm afraid. My father is ill, as Yusuf has determined. To rule in my stead, please help me by putting Yusuf in charge of the palace's affairs. He will take over until I see you again. You must be strong. I may not come home for some time. Yusuf has wanted me here, with my father dying. I don't want to be king, yet Yusuf does believe I must. Be brave!

Love,

Ahmed

Fatima sighed. "Seems clear to me."

Tansy and Lysandra nodded.

Elena jiggled a cooing Hassim up and down on her knees. "May I have a look?"

"Sure," said Fatima. She handed the letter to Elena, then reached for Hassim, who wailed when she plucked him from Elena's lap.

Elena's eyes scanned the letter once, then widened as she scanned it a second time. "I think that Ahmed was writing this letter in a kind of code!" she exclaimed. "By switching around a few commas and periods, the meaning changes completely. Listen:

"My dear Selime,
I am detained against my will. I'm afraid.
My father is ill. As Yusuf has determined to
rule in my stead, please help me. By putting
Yusuf in charge of the palace's affairs, he will
take over. Until I see you again, you must be

strong. I may not come home. For some time
Yusuf has wanted me here. With my father
dying, I don't want to be king yet. Yusuf does.
Believe I must be brave!

> *Love,*
> *Ahmed"*

When Elena finished reading the letter, the princesses stared at one another in alarm.

On the Trail

SELIME COLLAPSED ONTO A CHAIR. "IF ELENA IS right about the letter, Ahmed is in danger!" she cried. "The only way Yusuf can become king is if King Murad and Ahmed *both* die before Hassim is old enough to rule."

Lysandra shook her head. "I don't understand. Isn't Prince Ahmed at King Murad's palace? How could he be in danger there?"

Fatima frowned. "I don't know, but I'm

going to find out. Follow me, everyone. To the Crystal Ball Room!"

The Crystal Ball Room housed the palace's crystal ball, which could be used to look in on the Crystal Ball Room in any other palace or castle. If no one happened to be in the room, you could place a message in front of the ball to be read later.

With Selime carrying Hassim, the princesses hurried along one hallway and down another, past Ahmed's library. But when they reached the open doorway of the Crystal Ball Room, they gasped. The marble tabletop stood empty. The crystal ball was gone!

Footsteps sounded behind the princesses, and they turned around. Yusuf stood in the hallway. As they watched, he drew his sword.

Selime's cheeks flushed. "Just where is my crystal ball?" she demanded.

Yusuf smiled. Running a thumb over the

sword's blade, he said, "I'm afraid your crystal ball was looking a bit dull. I sent it away to be polished." He motioned toward her with the tip of his sword. His dark eyes narrowed. "What was the message you wanted to send? Must have been important for all of you to come at once."

Fatima bit her lip. He mustn't know they suspected he was up to no good! So, in a lighthearted voice, she said, "Oh, that's too bad. We asked Selime if we could have a party next week, and we wanted to send messages home to have our best dresses delivered."

Yusuf seemed to relax a little. "Ah—a splendid idea, but I'm afraid a party right now is out of the question."

"But why?" asked Lysandra, pretending to pout.

"Because next week I'm having the Grand Hall and the Ballroom completely remodeled."

Yusuf glanced quickly in Selime's direction. "I'm going to bring this palace up-to-date."

"How nice," said Selime, with faked enthusiasm.

That afternoon Selime kept Yusuf busy, pretending to be interested in his plans for remodeling. Meanwhile, the princesses holed up in Fatima's room, making their own plans. "We must find Ahmed," said Fatima, "before it's too late."

"Shall we travel to King Murad's palace then?" asked Tansy.

Fatima shook her head. "I'm not sure he's there."

"Where else would he be?" Tansy asked.

"I don't know," said Fatima. "But I suspect Yusuf is keeping him prisoner somewhere. I think he went to see Ahmed last night That's why he took food from the kitchen."

Elena nodded. "Exactly what I was thinking."

"But there are four of us," I____
reminded them. "Five with Selime.
overpower Yusuf—maybe tie him u____
we can force him to tell us where Al____

Fatima thought about Yusuf's sha____
"Even if we could capture him, he'd____
And we're not completely sure we____
anyway." She paused to think. "I sa____
with our earlier plan and follow him____
sneaks out tonight."

"If he sneaks out tonight," said ____

"Right," they all agreed.

That night the princesses kept wato____
from Fatima's window. Midnight____
went, and still they hadn't seen hi____

"Maybe he left the palace a dit____
Lysandra said after a while.

"Or maybe he's not leaving a____
said Tansy.

Fatima had to admit that either scenario was possible. Still, she tried not to let herself think the worst—that there was no need for Yusuf to bring food because Ahmed was already dead.

Finally, however, they heard a soft whinny, and Yusuf's black stallion appeared from around the side of the palace. In a few more minutes, Yusuf came out with a bundle, stuffed it into his saddlebag, and was off.

The princesses wrapped cloaks around their clothes, then swooped through the open window on Fatima's carpet. The moon lit their way as they followed Yusuf. His horse skirted the village and galloped into the countryside. As she flew above an olive orchard, Fatima saw Yusuf glance over his shoulder at the sky. Her heart beating fast, she skimmed behind a tree, hoping he hadn't seen them. If he had, she hoped he'd mistaken them for some strange, large bat. After a while, when he didn't stop or turn back, the girls continued to follow.

They'd been traveling for nearly two hours when they came to a desolate place with scrubby trees and a few crumbling buildings. "Looks like an abandoned village," whispered Elena.

"Whoa!" said Yusuf, reining in his horse. He dismounted, pulled the bundle from his saddlebag, and strode over to what looked, from above, like a round circle of stones.

"I brought you some food, Ahmed!" he yelled, tossing the bundle down. "But if you don't do as I ask, it's the last you'll get."

Fatima gasped. "It's a well," she hissed to the others. "Yusuf is keeping Ahmed in a well!" She lowered the carpet behind one of the crumbling buildings where they could watch without being seen.

Now Ahmed's voice echoed from the bottom of the well. "You slimy worm!" he cried. "You son of a dung beetle! God knows, I

don't want to be king yet, but I'll never give up the throne to you!"

"Then you've made your choice!" yelled Yusuf.

Mounting his horse, he sped away as Ahmed continued to hurl curses. "You mealy-mouthed maggot! You pimple on the face of the earth!"

Fatima couldn't help smiling. She never would've guessed that her own brother-in-law, who scolded *her* for cursing, was an expert at it!

After waiting a few minutes to make sure Yusuf wasn't going to return, the princesses approached the well and peered over the edge.

"Ahmed!" Fatima called into the dark hole. "It's me, Fatima! My friends and I have come to rescue you!"

The Rescue

"It's about time!" Ahmed yelled from the bottom of the well. "What took you so long?"

Fatima sighed. She supposed it was asking too much to expect a little gratitude. For a second she thought about leaving him there!

Since there was no ladder nearby and since the well opening was small, Fatima rolled up her flying carpet and dropped it down to Ahmed. It hit him on the head.

"Ouch!" he yelled.

"Sorry!" Fatima called.

Ahmed didn't own a flying carpet, and he'd never been very good at flying one. "Oof! "Ow!" he exclaimed all the way up as he bumped against the sides of the well.

After Ahmed was out, Elena doctored his scrapes and bruises, dabbing them with a creamy white lotion from a small blue bottle. The lotion was magical, and Ahmed's wounds healed instantly. He took no notice, however.

"Yusuf tricked me," Ahmed explained to the girls. "On our way to my father's palace, he suggested we take a shortcut. When we reached this abandoned village, he pretended to be lost. Then he suggested we check the well for water since our supply was getting low."

Ahmed rubbed his forehead. "I should've been suspicious, but I wasn't. He lowered me over the side of the well with a rope. I told him the well was dry. But he just laughed, then yanked up the rope so I couldn't get out."

"Of all the low-down, dirty rotten tricks," muttered Tansy.

"That's for sure," said Lysandra.

Fatima nodded. "And then he demanded you give up your right to be king!"

"That's right. He wanted me to sign a paper renouncing my claim—and Hassim's future claim—and naming *him* king." Ahmed frowned. "Can you imagine Yusuf in charge of the kingdom?"

Fatima shuddered, thinking of the many servants he'd already fired and the changes he was planning to make to the palace. "Elena figured out the message you sent," she said.

Ahmed sniffed. "Well, I'm glad *someone* did!"

Bats and bullfrogs! It was *impossible* to please him. And he hadn't even thanked Elena for healing his wounds. But if Elena minded, she didn't show it.

Crowding onto Fatima's carpet, the five of them started back to the palace. Along the way, Fatima filled in Ahmed on all that had happened at the palace the last few days.

"How could my own cousin turn out to be such a fiend?" Ahmed muttered.

"I know how you feel," Lysandra said sympathetically. Fatima guessed she must be thinking about her cousin Owen. A whiny boy, with a large chin and beady eyes, he was always threatening to reveal Lysandra's secrets unless she gave him coins from her magical purse. Yusuf was certainly more handsome than Owen, but Fatima had to wonder if he'd behaved like Owen when he was younger. It made her blush to think how they'd all been deceived by Ahmed's charmingly clever cousin.

The sky had begun to lighten, and daybreak was upon them when they reached the palace. Fatima brought the flying carpet to a halt. Hastily she rolled it up, then burst through the doors with the others. A horrible sight met everyone's eyes.

Yusuf stood halfway up a long, steep staircase leading to a tower. Under his arm he clutched a wailing, kicking bundle. *Hassim!*

Dressed in her nightgown, her hair streaming wildly about her face, Selime screamed, "Give me back my baby!"

Ahmed ran to her, and the two of them started up the stairs.

Yusuf drew his sword. The blade glinted sharply. "Don't come any closer or you'll be sorry," he snarled.

Selime fainted into Ahmed's arms.

Thinking quickly, Fatima whispered to Lysandra, "Give me your purse!"

Without a word, Lysandra whipped her purse from around her neck and handed it over.

Fatima ran a few steps forward, waving the purse high so Yusuf would see it. "I'll trade you this purse for Hassim!" she shouted.

"Ha!" spat Yusuf. "What would I want with a purse when I can have a whole kingdom?"

"Watch!" Fatima motioned to Lysandra, who hurried forward. Lysandra held her purse upside down and showered the floor with far more coins than one small purse could possibly hold.

Yusuf's eyes gleamed with greed at the sight.

Lysandra closed the purse and tossed it to Fatima, who waved it in the air again. "It's a magical purse," she called to Yusuf. "It never goes empty!" Of course, she didn't tell him that the magic only worked for the purse's true owner. If anyone but Lysandra so much as opened it, he or she would get a very nasty surprise.

"With this purse you'll be able to *buy* yourself a kingdom!" Fatima yelled. "A dozen kingdoms if you'd like. Just think of all the castles and palaces you can remodel. You won't *need* Ahmed's inheritance."

"Good idea," Yusuf called down. He mumbled a few words and Fatima felt her grasp on the purse loosen. Magically it rose in the air and began to float toward Yusuf.

"No!" Fatima lunged for the purse and caught it. She held onto it tightly. "I said I'd *trade*."

Yusuf rolled his eyes. "All right. We'll trade." With Hassim still clutched under one arm, whimpering, Yusuf came down the stairs. He waved Ahmed away with his sword as he passed. "Move!" he shouted to the other princesses as he approached Fatima. They scurried out of his way.

Fatima tucked the purse under one arm while she reached for Hassim. Shoving the baby at her, Yusuf grabbed the purse, then bolted out the front doors of the palace.

The Capture

To Fatima's surprise, Hassim stopped crying at once. His mouth crinkled into a smile as he stared up at her. Beaming back at him, Fatima kissed the top of his head. It was starting to be covered by fine black hairs, she noticed, and didn't look so much like a squashed pumpkin anymore.

Selime had recovered from her faint. She and Ahmed rushed over, and Selime took

Hassim into her arms. With tears running down her face, Selime hugged Hassim tight. "My baby! My darling!" she cried.

Hovering over them, Ahmed cooed, "Oh, my sweet little baby waby. My own little princey wincey."

For once the baby talk didn't make Fatima feel like gagging. She was just glad Hassim was safe and sound. Standing together a few feet away, the other princesses caught Fatima's eye and smiled.

Prince Ahmed stopped fussing over Hassim. He smacked his forehead. "What's the matter with me! We need to catch Yusuf. We need to get Lysandra's purse back!"

Before Fatima could explain that going after Yusuf wasn't really necessary, a scream loud enough to be heard two kingdoms away sliced the air like a sword. The princesses began to giggle.

Lysandra grinned. "I think Yusuf just opened my purse."

Following the screams, Ahmed and the princesses raced outside to the back of the palace. They arrived just in time to see a swarm of angry bees chase Yusuf into the lake. When he came up, gasping for air, the bees dove down to sting him again. "Help!" he screamed.

Spotting her purse lying open on the ground, Lysandra picked it up and closed it tight. Instantly the bees flew straight up into

the sky and disappeared.

Prince Ahmed fished his cousin out of the lake. Yusuf was covered with nasty red welts and blubbering louder than Hassim on his worst day. "I only wanted to improve things!" he cried. "I only wanted to show how well *I* could run a kingdom!"

"Right," Ahmed said grimly. Clapping his strong hands around Yusuf's arms, he pulled him toward the palace.

"You understand me, don't you, Fatima?" Yusuf whined as he passed her. "You've always liked me. If you talk to Ahmed, I know he'll let me go."

Fatima only stared at him. She had no sympathy for him anymore.

Yusuf fell silent. His upper lip curled and he glared at Fatima with a look of stone-cold hate.

Fatima shivered. Yusuf didn't look so handsome now that his face was swollen from bee stings and his hair and clothes were dripping wet. To think she'd ever wished Ahmed could be more like *him*!

Ahmed locked Yusuf in the tower for safekeeping. He asked the guards to keep careful watch so that Yusuf couldn't use magic to escape. Then he joined the princesses for breakfast in the Grand Hall. "Thank you for everything you've done for me and my family," he said as he sat down at the table. "I can only apologize for my cousin's wicked behavior."

"That's okay," said Lysandra. "I know all about rotten cousins."

"And I've got six brothers," said Tansy. "They may not be as wicked as Yusuf, but they can still make life pretty miserable sometimes."

"We were glad to help," Elena said.

"Yusuf may be your cousin," Fatima told Ahmed, "but he's nothing like you. He's a slimy worm, and a mealy-mouthed maggot, and . . . and a son of a dung beetle!"

"Really, Fatima!" Ahmed exclaimed. "I've told you how I feel about cursing. Wherever did you hear such . . ." He stopped talking and, slowly, his face turned red. "Oh. I guess you must have heard *me*."

The princesses giggled.

"Yes. And I completely agree with you," said Fatima. "Furthermore, I think Yusuf deserves the worst punishment you can think of."

"So do I," said Ahmed, reaching for a platter of scrambled eggs. "That's why I'm sending him home to his mother, right after I eat."

"What!" said Fatima. "What kind of punishment is that?"

Ahmed spooned egg onto his plate. "Ah, but

you don't know my aunt. She'll be angrier than those bees when she finds out what Yusuf's been up to. *I* wouldn't want to face her."

"What about King Murad?" Elena asked. "Do you think he's as ill as Yusuf said?"

Prince Ahmed's brow wrinkled with worry, and his shoulders sagged. "I'm afraid he may be. Otherwise, why would Yusuf have tried so hard to steal my inheritance?"

Fatima was worried too. It was the same thought she'd had. For Ahmed's sake, she hoped Yusuf was wrong.

A Journey

FATIMA PULLED AWAY FROM THE TABLE AND stood up. "We should go see your father at once!" she exclaimed.

Ahmed set down his fork. *"We?"*

"Of course," said Fatima. "My flying carpet will get us there much faster than a horse. And you'll need me to fly it."

Ahmed opened his mouth as if to object, then closed it. "You're right," he said. "But what about your friends? You can't just leave them here alone."

"Of course she can," said Tansy. "Besides, Selime and Hassim will be here."

Lysandra nodded in agreement. "We'll be fine."

"I'd like to go with Prince Ahmed and Fatima," Elena said softly. "In case I can help."

"Good idea," said Fatima, but she wondered how useful Elena's magical lotion would be if King Murad was seriously ill.

When Ahmed finished eating, he sent word to town to rehire all the servants Yusuf had dismissed. Then he sent two men to fetch Yusuf from the tower. As he was being put into a carriage, Yusuf tried to twist away from the guards. "I hate you!" he yelled over his shoulder at Ahmed. "Why did you have to tell my mother?"

Ahmed chose not to reply. The guards

shoved Yusuf into the carriage and climbed in after him. They would accompany Yusuf to his mother's home to make sure that he didn't escape.

Meanwhile, Fatima and Elena prepared for the journey to King Murad's palace. While they were deciding what to take, Nar appeared in the doorway. She twisted the tip of her pigtail. "I just wanted to say thank you," she said shyly. "I'm so happy to have my job back."

"You're welcome," said Fatima. "I guess you know about Yusuf by now."

Nar nodded. "All the servants are glad he's gone." She reached behind her and picked up a large bag. "This is for you," she said. "For your journey." After handing the bag to Fatima, Nar curtsied and left.

"What's in it?" Elena asked.

Fatima opened the bag and they peered

inside. It was filled with all sorts of good food—meats and cheeses, bread and butter, oranges and grapes, and Fatima's favorite, honeyed stuffed dates.

After they'd said good-bye to the others, Fatima, Elena, and Ahmed flew off to see King Murad. Fatima guided her carpet skillfully, skimming over trees and mountains, valleys and lakes. They reached King Murad's palace by nightfall.

Fatima brought the carpet to a gentle halt outside the palace. The intricately carved doors were immediately flung open, and a servant showed the visitors down a grand, candlelit hallway to the king's chamber.

King Murad lay in the dim room, sighing and groaning. Fatima and Elena lingered just outside the door, but Ahmed stepped up beside his father's bed. "It's Ahmed, Father. I've come to see you."

"Ahmed!" gasped King Murad. "You're here at last!"

Ahmed kneeled next to him and clasped one of his father's hands. "I would have been here sooner, but . . . well, we can talk about that later, after you're feeling better."

"Oh, my poor boy," King Murad moaned. "I'm afraid this time it is the end."

"Now Father," Prince Ahmed scolded lightly, "you mustn't talk like that."

"But just look at me!" said the king, pushing himself up against the pillows.

Ahmed reached for a candle flickering on the bedside table, next to a silver bowl of nuts. He held it over the king. Fatima heard Ahmed draw in his breath. "You look just like Yusuf did after . . ." His voice trailed off.

"Yusuf? What about Yusuf? Is he ill too?" asked the king.

"Never mind about Yusuf," said Ahmed.

"You haven't been stung by bees, have you? How long have you had these horrible red bumps?"

"Bees?" The king shook his head weakly. "No. It's a rash, and I've had it for more than a week." He groaned. "It's hot and itchy and getting worse. The doctors think it's the plague. They're afraid of catching it, so they examine me from a distance."

Fatima drew back a little, but Elena stepped into the room. "Excuse me, Your Majesty," she said, "but may I have a look?"

"Who's this?" The king sounded startled.

Fatima came forward. "I'm Selime's sister, Fatima. And this is my friend, Princess Elena." They both curtsied. "Elena is skilled at healing. Maybe she can help."

The king sighed. "I fear I'm beyond anyone's help." Then, managing a feeble smile, he added, "But where are my manners? You

must be hungry after such a long journey."
He motioned to the silver bowl on his
bedside table. "Won't you have some nuts?
They're about the only thing I've eaten
since I became ill. In fact, I'm feeling a little
hungry now myself. Maybe I'll have a few

too." He reached for the bowl, but Elena
stopped him.

"I think those nuts may be the problem,"
she said.

"What?" cried Ahmed. "You don't think
they're poisoned, do you?"

Could he be thinking the same thing she was? Fatima wondered. What if Yusuf . . . ?

But Elena shook her head. "No, nothing like that. But sometimes certain foods, such as nuts, can cause a rash. If I'm right, Your Majesty, you'll get better once you stop eating them. But for now," she said, uncapping her little blue bottle, "this lotion should help."

Back Again

WHEN FATIMA AND ELENA CAME DOWNSTAIRS for breakfast the next morning, King Murad was sitting with Ahmed, enjoying a huge meal of scrambled eggs, fruit, and pastries. King Murad beamed when he saw them. "The rash is gone!" he said. "I feel wonderful. Like I could go on living for another fifty years!"

"And I hope you shall, Father," said Ahmed.

Fatima and Elena looked at each other and smiled.

Later that morning Ahmed filled in his father on Yusuf's doings. The king shook his head sadly. "Disgraceful! His mother will be utterly enraged. Sending Yusuf to her is a just punishment indeed. And I'm so glad you're okay."

Shortly afterward Ahmed and the princesses left for home. As Fatima's carpet sailed over lakes and valleys, mountains and trees, Prince Ahmed praised Elena. "It was clever of you to figure out what was causing my father's rash when none of those doctors could." He rolled his eyes. "The plague, indeed!"

Jealousy surged through Fatima. She was proud of her friend too, but why couldn't Ahmed ever say anything nice about *her*?

It was evening when they finally arrived back at the palace. Ahmed went in search of Selime and Hassim, while Fatima and Elena ran off to find their friends.

"I can't believe how much has happened since we've been here!" Tansy said later as she polished her flute in Fatima's room.

Fatima stopped brushing Elena's hair. She'd been trying to take some of the frizziness out of it, but it only sprang back, frizzier than ever. "I'm afraid it wasn't exactly the adventure I'd hoped for."

Tansy looked up from her flute. "I thought the whole thing was rather exciting."

"Me too." Lysandra set down the book she'd been looking at. "Especially now that the dangerous parts are over."

"I like your family," said Elena. "And King Murad is nice, too."

Fatima raised an eyebrow. "And Yusuf?"

Lysandra shrugged. "Every family has at least one bad apple. At least Yusuf could tell good stories and perform great tricks."

Fatima nodded. She supposed everyone had good and bad in them, only sometimes the balance tipped more in one direction than the other. "Want to go to the bazaar before it closes?" she asked the others.

"Yes!" they all shouted together.

While her friends got ready to leave, Fatima went to tell Ahmed and Selime where

they were going. As she approached their room, she could hear Ahmed speaking. "I was wrong about Fatima," she heard him say.

"What do you mean?" Selime asked. Fatima held her breath and hid behind the door, wondering if Ahmed was going to say something awful about her.

"Remember how I told you I thought she

was too young and irresponsible to care for Hassim?"

Fatima's cheeks warmed. It was something *she'd* never forget!

"Well," said Prince Ahmed, "I take it all back."

Fatima almost fell over. He did?

"If it hadn't been for her and her friends," Ahmed continued, "I'd still be down at the bottom of a well. And Hassim . . . well . . . I'd prefer not to think about that. Have you seen the way she handles that carpet, by the way? She's amazing!"

"Have you told *her* that?" Selime asked.

Ahmed paused. "Not in so many words, I guess. It's hard for me to say these things sometimes. You know that, right?"

"Yes, dear. I do," said Selime. "But I love you anyway."

Smiling, Fatima entered their room. "I

came to tell you that my friends and I are going to the bazaar," she said.

"Okay," said Selime. "Have a good time."

"Be back before dark," Ahmed said gruffly.

"We will," said Fatima. Then, surprising both Ahmed and herself, she gave him a great big hug.

AND NOW FOR A SNEAK PEEK AT
Princess Power #3:
The Awfully Angry Ogre

Princess Tansy

PRINCESS TANSY WOKE WITH A START. SOMEONE was knocking on her door. "Just a minute!" she called out, pushing back the bedcovers. Tansy shivered in the chilly morning air that seeped through the cracks in her family's castle. Grabbing her faded robe, she wrapped it around herself tightly, then hopped across the cold stone floor to open the door.

Tansy's room was at the top of a tower.

1

She'd recently chosen the room to get away from her six brothers. Before she moved, they'd made her life miserable, teasing her and playing practical jokes, such as putting frogs and snakes in her bed. Fortunately, none of them liked climbing the narrow, winding staircase to her room, and only came up to fetch her for a meal or to deliver a message. Edward, her oldest brother and worst tormentor, refused to come up for any reason. That suited Tansy just fine.

Tansy scraped her door open. "Good morning, lazybones," said her brother Jonah. At fourteen, Jonah was five years older than Tansy. Even though he could be just as mischievous as the others, he was Tansy's favorite. Jonah painted the most beautiful pictures—especially of Mount Majesta, which towered over the family castle. A dozen of Jonah's paintings of the mountain hung in Tansy's room.

Rubbing the sleep from her eyes, Tansy said, "What are you talking about? It's early!"

Jonah grinned. Like Tansy, he was slim and freckled, with ginger-colored hair. Only he was about ten inches taller than Tansy, who hadn't yet reached five feet. "Early for you, maybe," said Jonah. "I've been up since dawn." Jonah often rose early. Sunrise was his favorite time to paint Mount Majesta.

"So, what's up?" Tansy stifled a yawn.

"Besides you and me?" asked Jonah. "No one else in this family, that's for sure. They're all still snoring away."

Tansy frowned. "Then why did you get me up?"

"Maybe I just wanted some company," Jonah said with a smile. He paused as if remembering something. "Oh yeah. And someone's trying to reach you through the crystal ball."

"Why didn't you say so right away?" Tansy pushed past him and started down the steps to the Crystal Ball Room. "Did you see who it was?" she called back over her shoulder.

"Some girl with wavy blond hair."

Princess Lysandra! Tansy hadn't seen her friend in a couple of months, though they'd chatted a few times. The last time they'd been together—along with the princesses Fatima and Elena—they'd stayed with Fatima's sister and brother-in-law in their fabulous marble palace. She could still picture the rich silk tapestries lining every wall, and the gorgeous lake and gardens. The visit had turned out to be quite an adventure.

Tansy wound down the steps to the ground floor, then raced to the Crystal Ball Room and squeezed inside. No bigger than a wardrobe, the room was mirrored on three sides to make it seem larger, and a fake fireplace had been painted on the fourth wall. Tissue flowers, vaguely resembling roses, sat in a vase on top of a fake marble-topped table. Anyone looking in on her family through the crystal ball would see this room, so her family tried to make it look nice. Still, Tansy doubted their efforts hid how poor they really were.

Lysandra's image floated in the ball. She was bent over a piece of paper, writing. Tansy had visited Lysandra's palace, so she knew nothing was fake about her family's grand Crystal Ball Room.

Lysandra glanced up. "Oh, hi," she said. "I didn't think you were in, so I was going to leave you a note."

"My brother Jonah saw you. He came and told me."

Lysandra's face moved closer to the ball. She squinted at Tansy. "You're in your robe, aren't you? Did I get you out of bed? I forgot about the time difference. It's two hours earlier where you live, isn't it?"

"That's okay," said Tansy. She hoped Lysandra couldn't tell how faded her robe was. She didn't like to ask her parents for a new one with the royal treasury at an all-time low. "What's up?"

"I'm bored out of my skull," Lysandra said with a sigh. "Things are so dull around here that I almost wish Gabriella hadn't gotten married and moved away. Even listening to her nag was something to do."

Tansy laughed. Gabriella was Lysandra's older sister. If given the choice, Tansy would take one nagging sister over six annoying brothers any day, but she didn't say so. Instead, she said, "We need to get together again soon."

Lysandra's face brightened. "Exactly what I was thinking. In fact, I already talked to Elena and Fatima, and we'd like to come visit you, if that's all right. We could even be there in a few days. Fatima offered to fly all three of us on her carpet."

"Fantastic!" Tansy exclaimed, panicking at the same time. Her family's small castle was an embarrassment compared with the grand castles and palaces of the other princesses. What would the girls think of the way Tansy lived? Still, she couldn't very well tell them *not* to come. That would be rude! Besides, she really wanted to see her friends. Tansy bit her lip. "I'd love for you to visit."

"Great," said Lysandra. "I'll contact the others. See you soon!"

As she edged her way out of the Crystal Ball Room, Tansy hoped having everyone come wouldn't turn out to be a big mistake.

Find out what happens to Tansy and her friends in the next Princess Power adventure!

Check [...] fabulous princess adventure!

Princess Power #1:
The Perfectly Proper Prince

Hc 0-06-078299-4
Pb 0-06-078298-6

Princess Lysandra finds sewing, napping, and decorating the palace to be extremely boring. She wants adventure! So when Lysandra meets Fatima, Elena, and Tansy, she couldn't be happier. But their first quest comes even sooner than expected, when they stumble upon a frog that just might have royal blood running through his veins.

HarperTrophy®
An Imprint of HarperCollinsPublishers

www.harpercollinschildrens.com